A first book of

Or
to
ten
and
down
again

Written by David Lloyd
Illustrated by Carolyn Dinan

PUBLISHED BY THE READER'S DIGEST ASSOCIATION LIMITED

Once upon a time
a big red balloon
appeared quite suddenly
in the clear blue sky.

P.C. Merryman
was the first person to see it.
"Stop that balloon!" he shouted.
The balloon stopped.
"That's that and no mistake," he
said, placing the balloon under
arrest.
But that was by no means that.

Up and away went the red balloon,
up and away went
number 1,   P.C. Merryman,
up into the clear blue sky.

Mrs Howdoyoudo
was out shopping
when she saw the red balloon.
"Goodness gracious!
Now there's a funny thing!" she
said, catching hold of the string.

Up and away went the red balloon,
up and away went
number 1,   P.C. Merryman,
number 2,   Mrs Howdoyoudo,
up into the clear blue sky.

Jimmy Lookatme
was in the playground
shouting
when the balloon came down.
"Me! Me! Me!" he kept yelling
from the top of the slide,
snatching and snatching
for the string
until he caught it.

Up and away went the red balloon,
up and away went
number 1,   P.C. Merryman,
number 2,   Mrs Howdoyoudo,
number 3,   Jimmy Lookatme,
up into the clear blue sky.

Tom Knockatthedoor
was making people happy
popping letters through letter-
boxes when the balloon floated
into sight.
"Blow me! What a whopper!" he
said, reaching up to pull the
string.

Up and away went the red balloon,
up and away went
number 1,   P.C. Merryman,
number 2,   Mrs Howdoyoudo,
number 3,   Jimmy Lookatme,
number 4,   Tom Knockatthedoor,
up into the clear blue sky.

Miss Lookalive
was waiting outside the school
gates when the balloon arrived.
"Late again!" she said,
taking the balloon by the string
to lead it into the schoolroom.

Up and away went the red balloon,
up and away went
number 1,   P.C. Merryman,
number 2,   Mrs Howdoyoudo,
number 3,   Jimmy Lookatme,
number 4,   Tom Knockatthedoor,
number 5,   Miss Lookalive,
up into the clear blue sky.

Granny Pickupsticks
never saw the balloon at all
until she tried to pick up
the piece of string
lying on the ground.
"Waste not, want not," she said.

Up and away went the red balloon,
up and away went
number 1,   P.C. Merryman,
number 2,   Mrs Howdoyoudo,
number 3,   Jimmy Lookatme,
number 4,   Tom Knockatthedoor,
number 5,   Miss Lookalive,
number 6,   Granny Pickupsticks,
up into the clear blue sky.

The Reverend Ian Heaven
was humming hymns in the
churchyard when the balloon
appeared beside him.
"Hum, hum, hum," he hummed,
reaching out his hand
to touch it.

Up and away went the red balloon,
up and away went
number 1,   P.C. Merryman,
number 2,   Mrs Howdoyoudo,
number 3,   Jimmy Lookatme,
number 4,   Tom Knockatthedoor,
number 5,   Miss Lookalive,
number 6,   Granny Pickupsticks,
number 7,   the Reverend Ian Heaven,
up into the clear blue sky.

Maurice Meatonaplate
was shouting wildly at a dog
when the balloon came.
"Shoo! Shoo! Shoo!" he shouted.
The dog ran away.
The balloon stayed still.
Maurice Meatonaplate
grabbed it firmly with both
hands.

Up and away went the red balloon,
up and away went
number 1,   P.C. Merryman,
number 2,   Mrs Howdoyoudo,
number 3,   Jimmy Lookatme,
number 4,   Tom Knockatthedoor,
number 5,   Miss Lookalive,
number 6,   Granny Pickupsticks,
number 7,   the Reverend Ian Heaven,
number 8,   Maurice Meatonaplate,
up into the clear blue sky.

Nurse Feelingfine
was taking off her hat and coat
when the red balloon
started tickling her ear with its
string.
"Funny little itch," she said,
scratching her ear
and the string
at the same time.

Up and away went the red balloon,
up and away went
number 1,   P.C. Merryman,
number 2,   Mrs Howdoyoudo,
number 3,   Jimmy Lookatme,
number 4,   Tom Knockatthedoor,
number 5,   Miss Lookalive,
number 6,   Granny Pickupsticks,
number 7,   the Reverend Ian Heaven,
number 8,   Maurice Meatonaplate,
number 9,   Nurse Feelingfine,
up into the clear blue sky.

Little Lucy Playpen
thought the red balloon
was just another of her toys.
"Goo, goo, goo," she said,
even though she was quite old
enough to speak properly.
She lay on her back
and caught the string between
her toes.

Up and away went the red balloon,
up and away went
number 1, P.C. Merryman,
number 2, Mrs Howdoyoudo,
number 3, Jimmy Lookatme,
number 4, Tom Knockatthedoor,
number 5, Miss Lookalive,
number 6, Granny Pickupsticks,
number 7, the Reverend Ian Heaven,
number 8, Maurice Meatonaplate,
number 9, Nurse Feelingfine,
number 10, Little Lucy Playpen,
up into the clear blue sky.

Up and away they went,
up and away,
up and away.

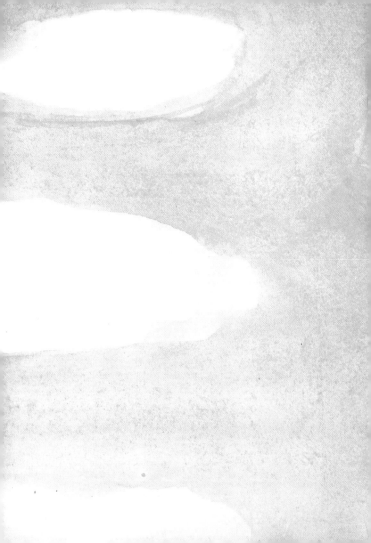

For as long as it takes to count
one to ten and down again,
there was nothing to be seen
in the clear blue sky
except little white clouds
slowly puffing by.

Then all of a sudden
down came tumbling
number 10, Little Lucy Playpen.

Down came tumbling
number 9,   Nurse Feelingfine,
number 8,   Maurice Meatonaplate.

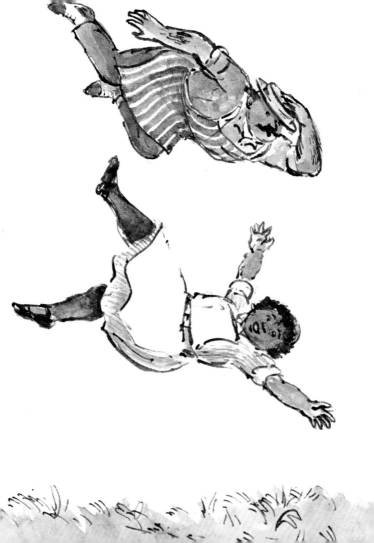

Down came tumbling
number 7,   the Reverend Ian Heaven,
number 6,   Granny Pickupsticks,
number 5,   Miss Lookalive.

Down came tumbling
number 4,   Tom Knockatthedoor,
number 3,   Jimmy Lookatme,
number 2,   Mrs Howdoyoudo.

Last of all
down came tumbling
number 1,   P.C. Merryman.

And although everyone
had tumbled to the ground
from a great height,
no one was hurt at all.

Sometimes
even a big red balloon
just can't help smiling.

MY FIRST LIBRARY

First Edition Copyright © 1980
The Reader's Digest Association Limited,
Berkeley Square House, Berkeley Square,
London W1X 6AB
Reprinted 1995

Copyright © 1980
The Reader's Digest Association
Far East Limited

Printed in Hong Kong